WHEN MOMS ATTACK!

WHEN MOMS ATTACK!

Adapted by Kim Ostrow

Based on the series created by Terri Minsky

Part One is based on a teleplay written
by Nina G. Bargiel & Jeremy J. Bargiel.

Part Two is based on a teleplay written
by Nina G. Bargiel & Jeremy J. Bargiel.

New York

Printed in the United States of America

13 15 17 19 20 18 16 14

Library of Congress Catalog Card Number: 2002101337

ISBN 0-7868-4538-4
For more Disney Press fun, visit www.disneybooks.com
Visit DisneyChannel.com

Lizzie McGUiRE

PART ONE

CHAPTER ONE

A tornado of clothing flew around Lizzie McGuire's room. Her jeans lay in a heap at the foot of her bed. Sweaters and sweatshirts lounged across her computer monitor. Even Lizzie's T-shirts hung off the lamps. It could have been declared a federal disaster area, but Lizzie paid no attention. She was way too busy searching through her drawer for the perfect pair of socks. When she finally found them, she shoved them into her purple backpack along with the rest of her "camping gear."

i know what you're thinking. But i have this situation totally under control. i've been packing for the overnight science trip since, like, last year.

Lizzie packed her favorite jeans, then reached for her pajamas with the pink ducks. She hesitated—did she really want her entire class to see her in those duckie pajamas? Maybe not, Lizzie decided, tossing them in the reject pile. As she combed her unmade bed for last-minute outfit choices, Lizzie picked up her soft but tattered favorite stuffed animal, Mr. Snuggles.

"Sorry, Mr. Snuggles," Lizzie said, placing him back safely on his side of the bed. "I'd never live it down if I brought you."

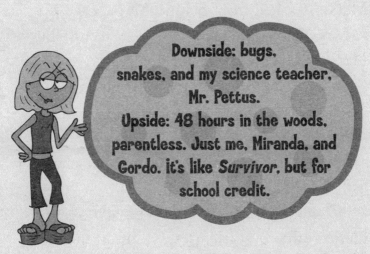

Downside: bugs, snakes, and my science teacher, Mr. Pettus.
Upside: 48 hours in the woods, parentless. Just me, Miranda, and Gordo. It's like *Survivor*, but for school credit.

Downstairs, the rest of the McGuire family sat around the breakfast table. Mr. McGuire was sharing the newspaper with Lizzie's mom. Lizzie's little brother, Matt, was eating a huge bowl of cereal and reading the back of the box. Lizzie needed a break from all her hard work, so she ran downstairs with her backpack to eat breakfast. The moment she set foot in the kitchen, the phone rang.

"Who would call during breakfast?" Mr. McGuire asked from behind his paper.

Mrs. McGuire went to pick it up, but Lizzie intercepted. "Hello?"

"Okay," her best friend, Miranda, said. There was no time for pleasantries. "Let's go over this one more time."

Miranda began to run through her checklist. "Flashlight?" she asked.

"Check," Lizzie and Gordo replied. Gordo, Lizzie's other best friend, was also on the line.

"Non-dorky pajamas?"

"Check," they responded. Lizzie heaved a sigh of relief as she walked out of the kitchen. She had made the right decision about the ducks.

Matt picked up the phone extension in the den. "Mom wants to know if you have batteries for your flashlight," he said.

"Mommmm!" Lizzie shouted. "Matt's on the phone!"

Mrs. McGuire ran into the den to take the phone out of her son's hand. "What are you doing? Respect your sister's privacy," she scolded. Then she put the phone to her ear. "Honey, do you have batteries for that flashlight?"

"Mom, I'm talking to my friends," Lizzie griped.

"I know that. I'm sorry," Mrs. McGuire said. She just couldn't help herself—she was even more excited about the camping trip than Lizzie was!

"Hi, Mrs. McGuire," Miranda and Gordo said in unison.

"You guys are gonna have the best time," Mrs. McGuire went on, "camping out, staying up late, telling ghost stories. I remember . . ."

Lizzie knew she had to come up with

something quick, or her mother would babble on all day. "Mom, there wasn't enough clean underwear for me to pack," she said, craftily.

"Oh, my!" Mrs. McGuire gasped. "Bye, guys!" There was a click as she hung up the phone.

"That was a brilliant ruse," Gordo congratulated Lizzie. She grinned.

"Hey, have you guys gotten 'The Talk' yet?" Miranda asked as she folded her favorite sweatshirt.

"You mean the 'Stick with Your Buddy' talk?" Gordo asked. His mom had just finished lecturing him at breakfast.

Lizzie sighed. "No, but I'm sure it's coming." She dreaded the moment she would have to hear all the dos and don'ts of camping from her mother. "See you on the bus?"

"If I don't get lost first," Gordo said with a laugh as he cleaned the lens of his video camera.

Miranda and Lizzie giggled and said good-bye.

Back in the kitchen, Mrs. McGuire was nosing through her daughter's backpack, comparing the contents against the school list she held in her hand.

"Mom, I'm old enough to pack myself," Lizzie said, walking into the room. "Plus, it's only overnight."

"I know, but it's not like you're going over to Miranda's house. I can't just swing by if you forget something." Mrs. McGuire's voice was muffled—her head was almost completely inside Lizzie's backpack. "You're taking this big step into a whole new world, and I just want to make sure you're fully prepared before I let you go. Remember to listen to your chaperone . . ."

"Mm-mm." Lizzie tried to make it sound as though she were listening. Here was "The

Talk" Miranda had warned her about. It was just as boring as she had feared it would be.

". . . and stick with your buddy," Mrs. McGuire added.

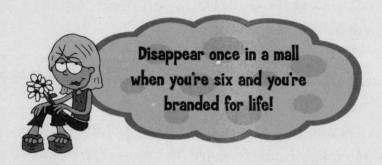

Disappear once in a mall when you're six and you're branded for life!

"Why can't *I* go camping?" Matt whined, pouring himself a second bowl of cereal.

Mr. McGuire put down his newspaper. "We'll camp this weekend with your Mom . . ." he said.

Matt's ears perked up. Finally—he was going to sleep in the great outdoors with bears and bugs and maybe a snake or two!

". . . in the house," Mr. McGuire added, turning back to his paper.

Matt slumped in his chair and kicked the table leg. "But it's not the same," he protested. "I mean, you won't even let me light a campfire in the living room."

"I know," Mrs. McGuire agreed, mussing Matt's hair. "Dad is such a wet blanket."

When Mrs. McGuire finished rummaging through her daughter's backpack, she made a very important discovery. "Honey, you don't have any toilet paper in here."

Lizzie blushed. "Mom, it doesn't say to pack any toilet paper on the list."

if humiliating me were an Olympic event, my mother would take home the gold.

"Well, you can't go to the woods without toilet paper." Mrs. McGuire's voice was matter-of-fact. Clearly, she had no idea how embarrassing this conversation was for Lizzie.

Lizzie rolled her eyes and clamped her mouth shut. She couldn't wait to get out into the woods. She was sure that there was nothing in nature remotely as embarrassing as her mother.

CHAPTER TWO

After school, Lizzie, Miranda, and Gordo sat around the lunchroom, waiting to board the bus. Their science teacher, Mr. Pettus, was supposed to be the chaperone, but he still hadn't shown up. Miranda and Lizzie discussed which outfits they had brought, while Gordo pulled out his video camera.

At that moment, Kate pranced into the lunchroom, wearing a camouflage sundress and matching sunglasses. She even had matching luggage—on wheels! Kate's best friend, Claire, was right behind her, as usual. Together, they ruled the school—and made Lizzie sick!

"Hey, Lizzie," Kate said in an obnoxiously sweet voice. "We were talking and wanted to know if you remembered to pack Mr. Snuggles."

Kate and Claire exchanged snide glances and laughed.

"Mr. Snuggles?" Lizzie asked innocently, as if she had never heard the name before.

"*You* know," Kate pressed. "Your fuzzy, little piggy you can't sleep without?" Lizzie bit her lip, knowing what was coming. "One time at a sleepover, Lizzie forgot Mr. Snuggles, and her mommy had to come over and drop him off," Kate said loudly, a smug smile on her lips.

Lizzie raised her eyebrows and shrugged

her shoulders. Part of her couldn't believe that she and Kate had ever been best friends.

"And you had those great pajamas, too," Kate went on sarcastically. "What were they? Pink puppies?"

Miranda stepped in to defend Lizzie. "They were ducks," she snapped, "not puppies."

Lizzie rolled her eyes. Miranda was *not* helping!

"Whatever," Kate said. "Did your mommy remember to pack your pink duckie pajamas? Or has she stopped shopping at Dorks 'R' Us?"

Gordo turned on his video camera. He focused on Kate, and zoomed in to the rescue. "So, Kate," he said in his best on-camera reporter voice. "Besides an F in science, what else do you expect to find in the woods today?"

Kate pointed her snooty nose up in the air

and said, "To tell you that, I'd have to talk to you. Which I don't." And with that, Kate and Claire pivoted on their platform sandals and walked away.

"I wonder if Spielberg started out this way," Gordo said with a sigh.

Lizzie grinned at him. "Thanks, Gordo."

"What about me?" Miranda put in eagerly. "I helped."

Lizzie folded her arms across her chest. "Yeah," she said, "you helped *her*. 'No, they were pink *ducks*. . . .'" Lizzie mimicked.

"I *tried*," Miranda insisted, tightening her ponytail.

Gordo secured his backpack and checked his camera one last time. He was on a mission to document this trip and he wanted to make sure that all of his equipment was working. "Well, I'm off to record adolescent milestones," he said. Lizzie and Miranda giggled as they watched their best friend head off into the sea of soon-to-be-campers, scouting for his next interview.

Mr. Pettus finally scurried into the lunchroom. "Okay, kids," he said, jamming his hands into the pockets of his white lab coat. "A final announcement before we load up the bus. There's a small problem with the girls' chaperone. Our own Mrs. Stebel ate some . . ." Mr. Pettus gave a nervous laugh. "Well, no need to bad-mouth the cafeteria. Don't worry, we don't have to cancel because we found a last-minute replacement."

Miranda leaned in close to Lizzie as Gordo rejoined them. "Ugh, I hope it's not Coach Kelly," she said. "I secretly think she and Mr. Booth the janitor are the same person."

"Or Mrs. Nagle," Lizzie added with a shudder. "She's got those weird teeth. I saw her eating lunch once. Scary."

"Whoever you get has got to be better than Mr. Pettus," Gordo said, pointing to the dorky science teacher's lab coat. "I put a frog in his pocket on Monday. Still there today."

Lizzie took Gordo's camera and zoomed in on the door to the lunchroom. "Well, let's see who our mystery chaperone is," she said, as the door opened and someone struggled to back into the lunchroom. All Lizzie could see was a humongous, geeky backpack spilling into the doorway.

"A big round of applause for the chaperone who has stepped in to save the day," Mr. Pettus said.

Lizzie watched the overgrown backpack wobble around the frame of the camera. This chaperone had to be a loser. Who on earth would pack so much junk in her backpack that she couldn't even stand up straight?

Mr. Pettus clapped wildly, trying to start a round of applause. "Everyone welcome . . . Mrs. McGuire!"

The camera dropped out of Lizzie's hands faster than she could say, "Mom!"

This is not happening, this is not happening, this is not happening. . . .

Mrs. McGuire bounded over to where Lizzie was sitting. "Hi, guys!" she sang, happy as a camper.

"Hey, Mrs. McGuire," said Gordo and Miranda.

For a moment, Lizzie couldn't speak—the humiliation was just too overwhelming.

"Mom, what are you doing here?" Lizzie finally managed to ask.

"Weren't you listening?" Mrs. McGuire said. "Mrs. Stebel ate in the cafeteria. . . ."

"I swear I won't get lost!" Lizzie pleaded, hoping her mother would disappear.

"Of course you won't get lost, honey. Because I'll be your buddy." Mrs. McGuire pulled her daughter into a bear hug. Finally, she noted the look of absolute panic on Lizzie's face. "And don't worry, I won't embarrass you," she added with a wink. "I'm a cool mom."

McGuire's a common name. Maybe people will think it's a coincidence.

Kate and Claire, unable to resist the lure of a chance to embarrass Lizzie, sauntered over. "Hi, Mrs. McGuire," Kate chirped. She was somehow able to kiss up and be snooty at the same time. It was enough to make Lizzie puke all over Kate's pedicure. "Did Lizzie forget to pack Mr. Snuggles again?"

"I'm afraid Mr. Snuggles wasn't invited," Mrs. McGuire said smoothly. "But I remembered to bring enough toilet paper for everybody!" And with that, she hoisted up a huge mesh bag filled to the brim with mounds of toilet tissue.

Guess what? You *can* die of embarrassment.

CHAPTER THREE

It was dinnertime, and Mr. McGuire and Matt were back in the kitchen.

"Where's Mom?" Matt asked.

"On the field trip with Lizzie," Mr. McGuire replied.

"Mom's chaperoning Lizzie's field trip?" Matt's eyes were wide. "Lizzie's gonna hate that." He thought for a moment, then added, "Cool!"

"It's just us men," Mr. McGuire said.

Matt beat his chest with his fists. "Men, men, men, men . . ." he chanted in a deep voice.

"Son." Mr. McGuire held up a hand, and Matt stopped chanting. "Why don't we see what Mom's left us for dinner?"

Together, the "men" opened the fridge and retrieved a wrapped dish from the top shelf. Slowly, they peeled off the top of the foil-covered mystery meal. When they saw—and smelled—what was under there, they jumped back in horror.

"It's that tuna-noodle casserole she's been trying to get us to eat for the past three weeks," Matt said, holding his nose.

"Oh, man." Mr. McGuire shielded his eyes and nose from the horror. "That's just plain mean."

Together, the McGuire men read the instructions Mrs. McGuire had left taped to the foil. A scrawled note said to heat at 350°F for twenty minutes.

"I don't think heating it up is gonna help," Mr. McGuire said, pointing to the instructions. "That's just gonna make it angry."

Matt's knees starting knocking. His teeth chattered as he bit his nails. "We're gonna starve, aren't we, Dad?" he asked. "It's gonna be like that movie where those people starved, isn't it?"

"We're not gonna starve, son," Matt's father assured him.

"We're not?" Matt asked nervously.

"No, son," Mr. McGuire said confidently. He put his hands on his son's shoulders and looked him in the eye. "We're gonna cook!"

"Aaaaaaaaaaargh!" Matt screamed. "We're gonna starve! We're gonna starve!"

"Don't you worry your spiky little head, son." Mr. McGuire patted Matt's gelled hair. "I have it all under control."

Matt stared deep into his father's eyes. Mr. McGuire gave Matt his best fatherly look to let him know everything would be all right. "We're gonna starve," Matt said with a sigh.

Meanwhile, far away from the comforts of home, the bus arrived at the campground. All the students shuffled out and gathered around Mr. Pettus. Lizzie wondered why he was still wearing his lab coat. She also wondered how far away from her mother she could stand before Mrs. McGuire would actually notice.

"The object of this afternoon's hike is to identify and classify as many species of plants and animals as possible," said Mr. Pettus, excited to deliver the day's mission. "We're going to split up into two groups: the girls, led by Mrs. McGuire, will be the Tagi."

At the mention of her name, Mrs. McGuire pumped her arm in the air. Lizzie cringed.

"And the boys," he continued, "led by myself, will be the Pagong. The group that identifies the most species of plants and animals will not have to eat a rat for dinner."

Mr. Pettus paused a moment. The students stared at him. "I'm kidding, of course," he added, but no one laughed.

Mr. Pettus reached into his pocket for a pen, but pulled out the frog Gordo had left for him the week before. "Hmm . . . must have jumped into my pocket when I got off the bus." Mr. Pettus looked confused and placed the frog on the ground. The frog didn't move. "He must be nocturnal," the science teacher said. "Anyway, the winners get to relax after the hike while the losers get to dig up earthworms with me for the class worm farm. Any questions?"

Kate raised her manicured hand high in the air, a look of disgust on her face.

Mr. Pettus shook his head, as if he knew what was coming. "Yes, Kate?"

"You don't mean worms from the ground?" Kate asked. "Do you?"

"Yes, Kate." Mr. Pettus's voice was patient. "Worms from the earth. *Earth. Worms.*"

Kate shuddered. Then she asked if she could bring a doctor's note on Monday to be excused from the activity. Mr. Pettus put his head in his hands and took a deep breath. He then repeated to the entire class that the only way not to have to dig up worms was to be in the group that identified the most plants and animals.

"Okay, everybody, let's go," Mr. Pettus announced. "Pagong, follow me!"

The boys trooped off after their teacher, heading deep into the woods. The girls gathered around Mrs. McGuire.

Kate was the first to speak, of course. "Mrs. McGuire, we better not lose," she said firmly. "I am *so* not digging for worms."

Lizzie's mom nodded. "That means we *so* need to win," she said. Lizzie cringed for the millionth time that day, and wondered if it were possible for her mother to be any less cool. She didn't think so.

"Okay, girls. WHO ARE WE?" Mrs. McGuire cried.

Nobody replied.

"And you guys go, *TAGI!*" Mrs. McGuire explained.

One or two of the girls mumbled, "Tagi."

Mrs. McGuire didn't lose heart. "WHAT ARE WE GONNA DO?" she cheered.

Blank stares.

Clearly, these girls needed a lesson or two in spirit. "Then you go, *WIN!*" Mrs. McGuire shouted.

"Win," the girls said weakly.

"Okay, then." Mrs. McGuire decided that was enough camp spirit for now. She figured the girls would turn around soon enough, once they started identifying all of the thrilling flora and fauna that surrounded them.

Lizzie's mom led the troop into the forest, but Lizzie hung back for a minute. She needed a second to deal with the fact that her mom was a supergeek. No question about it.

Tonight, on LizzieVision:
When Good Moms Go Bad!

Once they were deep in the woods, Mrs. McGuire and the girls spotted a bird high up in a tree. Miranda flipped through the guidebook, hoping to identify it quickly. She wanted to locate as many species of animals as possible so she could get out of her hiking boots—*and* out of digging up gross earthworms.

"I was right!" Miranda said, closing the book. "It *is* a yellow-bellied sapsucker!"

"Excellent job!" Mrs. McGuire held up her hand. "High five, girlfriend!"

My mom just high-fived my best friend. And the worst part is she actually thinks she's being cool.

CHAPTER FOUR

Meanwhile, back at the McGuire kitchen, things were definitely cooking. Mr. McGuire was studying *The Complete Idiot's Cookbook*, reading off a checklist of ingredients to Matt. "Salt?" he asked.

"Got it," Matt said.

"Half dozen oranges?" Mr. McGuire continued.

"Got it!" Matt tossed an orange in the air and caught it, cheered on by an imaginary crowd.

"One whole duck?" asked Mr. McGuire, his head buried in the pages of the cookbook.

"*No* got it." Matt opened the freezer and checked inside. "We've got hamburgers and Fudgsicles."

Mr. McGuire thought for a moment, then checked the recipe one more time. "Duck isn't totally necessary for duck à l'orange," he assured his son. "We'll improvise. The best chefs in the world think on their feet."

Matt stared at the oranges on the counter. "I've got a bad feeling about this," he said, putting his head in his hands.

Meanwhile, Mrs. McGuire was still carrying on about the yellow-bellied sapsucker. After all, this trip was supposed to be educational, and Mrs. McGuire took her job as a chaperone very seriously. Unfortunately, by the time she finally finished reading about the yellow-bellied sapsucker to her troop, the girls were all yawning and fighting to stay awake.

They groaned and struggled to their feet. Mrs. McGuire plowed ahead, her troop trudging behind her. "Wow, it's really quiet," Mrs. McGuire said, noticing the sound her feet made on the fallen leaves. "It's too quiet."

Lizzie listened hard, but she couldn't hear anything but the sound of her troop mates' breathing. The girls looked at one another with worried faces. Suddenly, a twig snapped behind Lizzie. She whipped around.

"Is anybody there?" she called.

Nothing. And then—

"PAGONG!" A pack of boys descended on them, armed with Super Soakers! The boys showed no mercy—high-pitched squeals echoed throughout the forest, as Gordo and the rest of the boys soaked every girl in the class. The boys didn't stop until they ran out of water. Lizzie stood, her fists clenched, dripping from her pigtails to her hiking boots. Slowly, she turned to Gordo.

"How . . . could . . . you . . . do . . . this?" she demanded through superclenched teeth.

"I'm getting in touch with my hunter-warrior instincts," Gordo replied proudly.

"Gordo!" Lizzie snapped.

Gordo looked sheepish. "Survival of the fittest?" he tried.

"Gordo!" Lizzie growled.

"It was Ethan's idea?" he suggested weakly, pointing to his classmate.

"Ahhhhhhhhhh!" Lizzie cried. Gordo took one look at her and ran. Lizzie was hot on his heels.

"Don't leave your buddy!" Mrs. McGuire called.

* * *

That night, the girls moped in their tent. They were sweaty, and dirty, and completely defeated. As they picked dirt from under their fingernails, the girls stared at the cans filled with mud and earthworms that sat before them.

"That was so unfair," said Lizzie, squeezing mud out of her hair. "How could we identify anything? Our guidebooks were soaked!"

"Mr. Pettus should have disqualified them," Miranda agreed, pouring mud out of her shoe.

"That was the grossest thing I have ever done," Kate said weakly.

Miranda shook her head. "I can't believe I touched a worm."

"Try hundreds of worms," Lizzie corrected her. "Gross doesn't even begin to cover it."

"It's your mother's fault," Kate said. "She's a terrible leader." She picked at her chipped nail polish, then held up her hands to show them to the girls. "What a waste of a manicure."

"It doesn't matter whose fault it was," Miranda said. "The point is, we have to get back at the boys. Any ideas?"

Lizzie stared at the disgusting cans filled with dirt and creepy worms. "Earthworms," she said, her eyes glued to the cans, "in their bunks."

Around her, the other girls' eyes lit up. Until—

"Absolutely not, Lizzie," Mrs. McGuire announced, stepping into the girls' tent.

At 6:27 P.M. on Friday night, my mother destroyed what was left of my life.

"There's no way we're putting earthworms in the boys' bunks tonight," Mrs. McGuire informed her troop. The girls all moaned in disappointment. But Lizzie was too furious to moan.

Forget the boys. Mom's getting earthworms in *her* bunk tonight!

"Oh, yeah," Miranda agreed, thinking about the plan a little more. "Someone's gonna have to take them in there. Do we really want to touch the worms again?"

Lizzie rolled her eyes. So what if her best friend had a point? She wasn't supposed to side with Lizzie's *mother*!

"Besides, boys *like* earthworms," Mrs. McGuire added.

"But we have to get back at them," Lizzie insisted. She paced back and forth around the bunk, wracking her brain to come up with a plan. "The only thing we have more of than earthworms is toilet paper. Maybe we should fill their bunks with toilet paper."

Mrs. McGuire began to smile. "Now, *that* is a great idea," she said.

Lizzie stared at her mother. "Huh?" she said.

Although Mr. McGuire and Matt weren't involved in a Super Soaker ambush, they were engaged in a mini-battle of their own. Dishes were piled high in the sink and on the counters. Pots and pans were strewn everywhere. The house reeked with a smell that could only be described as "science project gone bad."

Matt sat at the kitchen table, replaying what had happened in the past hour as they tried to make duck à l'orange. First, his father molded the ground beef to look like a duck. Then, Matt hacked off the fake duck's head so it would fit in the microwave. They crammed orange slices in around the beef, shut the door, and pressed START. That was when the microwave blew up, spewing fake duck and orange slices all over the kitchen. *Splat!* Matt doubted he would ever forget the horrible sound—or smell.

"We shouldn't have tried to make duck à l'orange," Mr. McGuire said morosely, eyeing the charred mess.

"Especially not with hamburger," Matt said.

"Y'know, the tuna-noodle casserole is sounding pretty good now," Mr. McGuire said, dreamily.

"That's the hunger talkin'," Matt reassured

his dad, bringing him back to earth. It was silent in the kitchen as the two McGuire men sat staring at each other. Then it hit Matt. "Dad, are we gonna die?"

The girls were all dressed in black, putting the finishing touches on their raid gear. Mrs. McGuire had donated her lipstick, so the girls would look just right. After all, a girl couldn't ambush the boys' bunk without the proper war paint! The tube of lipstick made its way down the line of girls. But when the lipstick got to Lizzie, she passed it to Miranda faster than if it were an earthworm.

"Okay, c'mon," Miranda said, painting her face. "Now *this* is fun."

"You wouldn't be saying that if it was *your* mom," Lizzie pointed out.

"My mom wouldn't lead a midnight T.P. raid on the boys' tent," Miranda countered.

"Okay, this is it." Mrs. McGuire was clearly excited to get started. She was dressed in black and wearing war paint, too.

Kate stood up. "Mrs. McGuire, are you gonna get us into more trouble?" she asked.

Mrs. McGuire paced back and forth in front of her troop, her hands clasped behind her back. "Yes," she said, "it *may* get you in trouble. Stay in the tent, and let the boys have their victory. Stay in the tent, and you may not get detention. Or you can follow me"—she held a roll of toilet paper aloft—"and T.P."

Miranda put on the finishing touches of her war paint and turned to Lizzie. "Here. Do your war paint," Miranda instructed.

"No! Are you kidding?" Lizzie snapped. "Stop encouraging her!"

"C'mon," Miranda urged, "if this were anyone else's mom, you'd be having the time of your life."

"Exactly," Lizzie agreed. "But it's not."

Lizzie gave the lipstick back to Miranda and turned her back. As far as Lizzie was concerned, this conversation was over. There was no way she was wearing war paint on her face, or having a good time.

"We have this *one* chance, this *one* moment to get back at the boys," Mrs. McGuire went on, rallying the troops. "Do not let your digging for earthworms be in vain." Mrs. McGuire stood tall. "Who are we?" she cried.

"Taaaagi!" the girls shouted.

"What are we gonna do?" Mrs. McGuire asked.

"WIN!" The girls pumped their fists in the air.

"Let's do this!" Miranda roared, totally psyched. The girls poured out of the tent and into the night. Lizzie had no choice but to follow. Still, she didn't have to act like she was enjoying herself, did she? She trailed behind the Tagi all the way to the boys' tent.

A few moments later, the girls were positioned outside the boys' tent. Mrs. McGuire handed out the rolls of toilet paper, making sure each girl got her own. On tiptoe, one by one, the troop members sneaked into the tent. First, they wrapped toilet paper around each bed. Some girls concentrated on wrapping the sleeping boys' feet, while others decided to place it around their heads. As the guys snored, some of the girls poured honey into their hair. The last few girls sprayed shaving cream on the floor—so when the boys got up, they would step right into a disgusting mess! It was the perfect payback for the water fight that earned them the revolting job of collecting squirmy earthworms.

But just as the girls were putting the finishing touches in place, a mysterious light shone through the tent. It took only a minute for the girls' fearless leader to realize they were totally busted.

"You guys, go!" Mrs. McGuire whispered to the girls. "Get out! Run back to the tent."

The girls hesitated, unsure what to do. Lizzie's mom made it easy for them by opening the tent flap and sending them on their way. "Back to the tent! Now! Save yourselves!" she said quietly as they hurried out.

The girls ran back to their tent as fast as they could. Meanwhile, in the boys' bunk, Mrs. McGuire was trying desperately to dodge the flashlight beam that was searching for guilty parties. She hopped to the left and jumped to the right—dancing around so that the light wouldn't fall on her. But in no time at all, the light landed right on her glasses. With toilet paper in one hand, and shaving cream in the other, Mrs. McGuire was caught—red-handed.

At the other end of the light stood Mr. Pettus. He wore red flannel pajamas, his lab coat, and a very disappointed look on his face.

"Mrs. McGuire?" he asked, confused. The sound of his voice woke the boys. As they stretched and yawned, they immediately knew something was wrong. Some guys struggled against the tightly wrapped toilet paper, others stepped in gooey gobs of shaving cream, and still others got their hands caught in their sticky, honey-coated hair.

Mrs. McGuire looked guiltily at Mr. Pettus and the boys. She gulped hard. Mr. Pettus stepped forward, triggering the rope that was attached to a surprise in the rafters.

Splat!

A water balloon dropped on his head! As it burst open, cold water drenched his messy hair. He did not look pleased.

"Tagi," Mrs. McGuire whispered weakly.

CHAPTER FIVE

Back at the McGuire house, Mr. McGuire and Matt were happily and hungrily chowing down on some pizza. It had taken a lot of work to get to this moment. Matt had a slice in one hand and a garden hose in the other. As he chewed, he filled up a kiddie pool with sudsy water. It was part of his brilliant plan for cleaning up the great McGuire duck à l'orange incident. Mr. McGuire was thrilled to be having a nice dinner with his son—and to erase the memory of flying ground beef and orange slices.

"Pizza's good. Got here quick, too," said Matt. "Dad, we gotta hang out more often."

Mr. McGuire looked at his son and nodded. It would be a long time before either of them tried cooking again.

The next day, the boys gathered their belongings and cleaned up the camp, looking rested and happy. After all, *they* weren't about to get into any trouble. The girls, on the other hand, were a wreck. Especially Lizzie. No one knew what their fate would be, but they suspected it would be . . . bad. Very bad.

"Detention for a year is the odds-on favorite," Gordo informed the girls.

Lizzie glared at him. "You're not helping," she said.

"This whole thing was your stupid idea,"

Kate snapped. "Your mom's gonna tell, and now we're all in trouble. Thanks, Lizzie."

"Well you did it, too," Miranda pointed out.

"Whatever," Kate said, then stormed off.

Once Kate was clearly out of earshot, Miranda sighed. "She's right," Miranda agreed. "We're so busted."

Gordo shrugged. "It happens."

Lizzie couldn't take it anymore. "No, I cannot get detention," she insisted. "People like me don't do well in detention. I'll never survive. It'll go on my permanent record, and I won't be able to get into college. I'll end up serving cones at the Dairy Freeze."

"I like those cones," Gordo protested.

Miranda and Lizzie stared at him icily.

"I'll be going now," he said, ducking away.

Mrs. McGuire marched over to the girls. They all huddled around her, quieting down to hear the news.

"Okay, kids, listen up," she said quickly.

"Mrs. McGuire," Miranda asked, "are we going to have detention forever?"

"Girls," Mrs. McGuire said, pushing her glasses up on her nose. "When you're an adult, you learn that all of your actions have consequences . . ."

"I knew it," Kate mumbled nastily. She shot Lizzie a dirty look.

Lizzie held her breath as Mrs. McGuire went on.

". . . and you have to live with those consequences, good or bad."

"It's gonna be bad. It's gonna be real bad," Miranda predicted, shaking her head. She sucked in her breath and prepared for the worst.

"But one good thing about being a kid is," Mrs. McGuire continued, "you have *parents* who can sometimes bail you out."

The girls looked at one another. What was Lizzie's mom getting at?

"So I told Mr. Pettus that I acted alone," Mrs. McGuire finished, her hand on her heart and her head bowed.

There was a beat of silence. The girls still didn't know what she meant.

"I took the rap," Mrs. McGuire told them.

The girls let out a collective sigh of relief— then a huge, roaring cheer for their awesome troop leader!

Okay, just when you're ready to trade her in for a new model, your mom does something cool. And you realize she's pretty much the coolest mom in the world.

Lizzie ran to her mother's side. "Mom," she said.

"What have I done now to annoy you?" Mrs. McGuire asked quickly, looking down at her daughter.

"Okay, I guess I've been a little hard on you," Lizzie admitted guiltily.

For the first time that weekend, Mrs. McGuire agreed with her daughter.

"Then I'm sorry," Lizzie said sweetly. "Because I'm really glad you made the trip."

"You are?" Mrs. McGuire asked.

"Yeah," Lizzie said. She was surprised to realize that it was true.

"I know having your mom along wasn't exactly what you had in mind for this weekend," Mrs. McGuire said, putting her arm around her daughter.

"Not exactly," Lizzie agreed. "But right now I think everyone kind of wishes you were their mom. And right now I'm really glad you're mine."

Mrs. McGuire was so excited she held her hand up to high-five her daughter. Lizzie quickly grabbed her mother's hand before she could raise it any higher. "High fives are *always* dorky, though," Lizzie informed her.

Mrs. McGuire's eyes grew wide. "Thank you," she whispered.

And then, as inspired by the best leader ever known to man, or at least to Lizzie and her class—Lizzie shouted, "WHO ARE WE?"

"TAGI!" the girls yelled back.

"WHAT'RE WE GONNA DO?" Lizzie asked.

"WIN!" the girls screamed.

Full of new confidence, Lizzie waltzed right over to Kate and Claire. Miranda followed. "I think you owe me an apology," Lizzie said to Kate, folding her arms across her chest.

Kate scoffed. "I don't owe you an apology," she said.

Lizzie thought for a second. "You're right," she agreed. "You owe my *mom* an apology."

Kate didn't say anything. She just gaped at Lizzie.

"Without my mom, this trip would have been canceled," Lizzie explained. "She dug up worms with us and then took the blame for something we all did. You owe her an apology."

Kate shook her head. "You're insane."

Lizzie stepped up close to Kate. "Whatever happened to the Kate I used to be friends with? The Kate I used to go to sleepovers with?"

Kate was still eyeing Lizzie as if she were wearing last year's shoes. Lizzie could tell from the expression on Kate's face that she had to try another way to make her see the light. It was time to pull out the serious stuff. "Or the

Kate whose pictures I have with her favorite teddy bear—what was his name? Mr. Stewart Wugglesby?" Lizzie taunted.

Kate turned nine shades of red. Claire gasped. Lizzie grinned.

"So," Kate said finally, staring at the ground, "where's your mom?" Lizzie pointed, and Kate went off to apologize. Lizzie and Miranda looked at each other and laughed. Not only did Mrs. McGuire just take the rap for them, but now Lizzie had gotten the best of Kate. It was the most perfect day.

The next Monday at school, Lizzie McGuire was a celebrity. Everyone wanted to talk to her in the hall. As she walked down the stairs, people patted her on the back or shook her hand. Lizzie basked in her newfound popularity. It was great!

At school, my mother was pronounced Coolest Mom Ever, of All Time, in the History of the Universe.

Miranda, Lizzie, and Gordo headed to math class together, just as they always did. But, today, Lizzie was on cloud nine.

"Hey, your mom could always lead next month's T.P. raid during the museum field trip," Gordo said, as they stood outside their classroom. "Is your mom chaperoning that?"

Lizzie flashed her friends a huge smile. "I don't think she'll be chaperoning for a while!" she said.

PART TWO

CHAPTER ONE

"Is there some sort of rule that every time it's raining we have to play dodgeball?" Miranda asked Lizzie.

Lizzie rolled her eyes. "It must be in the gym teacher guidebook," she said.

Gym class had just ended, and the girls were gathering their books at their lockers.

"Jennie Woods has a great arm," Miranda said, watching Jennie pull her books out of her locker, her muscles bulging like grapefruits. "She's like the Mike Tyson of dodgeball."

Lizzie nodded. Jennie Woods was small, but she was a dodgeball maniac. She could take down any one of Lizzie's classmates in a one-woman ambush. When she had finally nailed Lizzie in the back of the head, she did a ridiculous victory dance around the gym.

"She didn't used to be that way," Lizzie said, rubbing her head. "I mean, she plays the *oboe*! Oboe players aren't supposed to be violent."

"It's the bra." Miranda adjusted her pigtails and frowned at her reflection in her locker mirror. "Ever since she started wearing one, she's become a whole new person."

"Kind of like someone else we know," said Lizzie, staring down the hallway.

Miranda followed Lizzie's gaze to where Kate and Claire were prancing down the long hallway. They were the queens of mean and ultrasnobs—not to mention the most popular girls in school. Every she-geek within a ten-mile area bowed down before them. They made Lizzie want to puke.

She sighed. "Claire and Kate get a bra and become popular. Jennie Woods gets one and becomes Brandi Chastain."

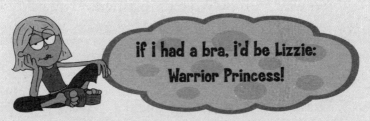

Miranda stared at Jennie Woods and her flat chest. "It's not like she even needs one," she whispered to Lizzie. "I mean, we need one way before Jennie does."

Lizzie cocked her head to one side and stared at her best friend. "So why *don't* we have one?" she asked.

"We *should* have one," Miranda agreed.

"You're right." Lizzie declared. "We're thirteen. It should be a rule."

Miranda checked herself out in her locker mirror again, just to make sure her fuzzy pink ponytail holders were even. Then she turned to Lizzie and said, "Ask your mom to give us a ride to the mall after school."

"No way!" Lizzie looked horrified. "You ask yours."

"I can't," Miranda said quickly. "She's working."

"Well, if we ask mine, she'll go with us," Lizzie pointed out.

Miranda bent down to lace up her boots. "How about we tell her we're shopping for school supplies?" she suggested.

"Miranda, you know I'm not good at lying," Lizzie said, pulling books out of her locker.

"Then *I'll* lie," Miranda said with a shrug. "She can just drop us off."

Lizzie stared down the hall. Kate and Claire were laughing hysterically at something— probably at one of their mean jokes, as usual. Could they *be* any more annoying?

"I guess that'll work," Lizzie said, hesitantly.

A plan this simple has to work. Right?

The school day went by faster than a great shoe sale at the mall. Lizzie was both nervous and excited. Miranda couldn't wait to start shopping! They talked about it all the way to Lizzie's house.

"Lizzie, is that you?" Mrs. McGuire shouted from the kitchen.

Just hearing her mother's voice made

Lizzie's knees start to shake. How was she going to get through this? "What do I say?" Lizzie asked Miranda, frantically.

"Yeah, Mrs. McGuire," Miranda said, rolling her eyes at Lizzie. "It's us!" Miranda's voice dropped to a whisper as she added, "Remember, not a word to your mom about the bra. We're going to the mall after school for *school supplies*. Repeat after me: *school supplies*."

"School supplies," Lizzie repeated. "Okay. School supplies, school supplies, school supplies." I can do this, Lizzie told herself as she and Miranda headed to the kitchen to start phase one of their foolproof plan.

Lizzie's mom stood at the kitchen table, folding laundry from a white plastic basket.

"Hey, Mrs. McGuire," Miranda said, taking a chocolate chip cookie out of the jar.

Lizzie stared at her. How could Miranda be

so calm at a time like this? Miranda elbowed Lizzie in the side.

"Hi, Mom," Lizzie squeaked.

"Hey, girls," Mrs. McGuire said, looking down at the laundry she was piling on the table. "How was school?"

"Fine!" Lizzie and Miranda said quickly—and at exactly the same time.

Mrs. McGuire looked up and stared at them quizzically for a moment. The girls looked back, smiles frozen on their faces. Lizzie was grinning so hard, her face was starting to hurt. "So, what's up?" Mrs. McGuire asked.

"Nothing!" the girls said together. Again!

Mrs. McGuire squinted at the girls. They smiled back. "Uh, Lizzie," she said, folding a T-shirt. "I have one more load of laundry to do. And I was thinking I might throw Mr. Snuggles in there, because he's looking a bit dingy."

Sweat started to pop out on Lizzie's forehead. She couldn't think about her stuffed pig at a time like this. She was supposed to be thinking about shopping and bras—not about her favorite stuffed animal.

"Uh, hello? Lizzie?" her mother said.

"Uh," Lizzie finally said. "I don't care what you do with Mr. Snuggles. Stuffed animals are for babies. Give him to Matt."

Mrs. McGuire stared at Lizzie. "But . . . you've had Mr. Snuggles since you were two. He's, like, your favorite toy."

Lizzie snorted and rolled her eyes. "*Was* my favorite toy, Mom. I don't need toys anymore. I'm an adult now." Lizzie stood tall and put her arm around Miranda's shoulder. "*We* are adults now."

Mrs. McGuire frowned and opened her mouth to say something, but Miranda cut her off. "So, Mrs. McGuire, could we have a ride to the mall?" she asked quickly.

Lizzie's mom shrugged. "Sure. What do you need?"

"School supplies," Miranda answered, shooting Lizzie a look.

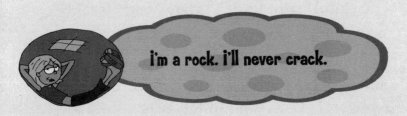

i'm a rock. i'll never crack.

"School supplies? Okay." Mrs. McGuire turned to Lizzie. "For what?" she asked eagerly, always interested in Lizzie's projects.

Lizzie's brain froze. "School supplies," she answered.

"Um, for a project," Miranda added.

"Okay," Mrs. McGuire said slowly.

Just then, the phone rang.

"Hold that thought." Mrs. McGuire picked up the phone. "Hello?"

When Lizzie's mom's back was turned, Miranda glared at her friend. "What *was* that?" she demanded, referring to the freak show her friend was suddenly starring in.

"School supplies?" Lizzie said weakly, shrugging her shoulders.

Miranda sighed. "Come on," she said, pulling Lizzie upstairs by the sleeve of her sweater. "Let's go put our books in your room before you totally spill your guts."

CHAPTER TWO

Mr. McGuire was reading the newspaper on the couch while Lizzie's younger brother, Matt, was jumping around the den, holding a magazine. Matt leaped over the back of the couch and plopped down right next to his dad. "See, I told you," Matt said, putting the magazine on top of the article Mr. McGuire was reading. "Jet Li is looking for a new side-kick for his latest movie."

Matt hopped off the couch and cleared his

throat. "The 'Untitled Jet Li Project'!" he crowed, sitting down and shaking his head. "Wow, what a great title."

Mr. McGuire folded up his newspaper neatly and gazed at his son with a look of concern. "Aren't you a little young for this?" he asked.

Matt pointed to the magazine and waved it around. "It says right here: ages ten and above."

Mr. McGuire took a look at the advertisement, hoping to find a loophole that would keep Matt out of the movies and in school! There didn't seem to be one, so when he heard Mrs. McGuire finish her phone call, he called her to the den. "Honey, what do you think about this?" he asked, giving her the magazine. Mr. McGuire stood behind his wife, reading the ad over her shoulder, and hoping she'd come up with a way out of this.

As his parents read, Matt began waving his

arms around and kicking his legs and making all the noises he had learned from all the martial arts movies he had watched. "*Hhhhhiiiyyyyyaaaa!*"

Mrs. McGuire read the ad aloud: "Your contest entry in the Jet Li Sidekick Sweepstakes can be a video, an essay, or even an audiotape."

She watched as her son karate-chopped the couch. "I think this is a terrible idea," she whispered to her husband. "I don't want him doing this."

The two watched as Matt tried to kick and chop anything in sight. But Mr. McGuire had finally figured out the best way to handle it. He leaned in close to his wife's ear and said, "Listen, he's not gonna win, so we don't have to tell him no. Someone else will. Meanwhile, we get the credit for being really cool parents."

"I think it's a great idea, honey," Mrs.

McGuire told Matt enthusiastically. "Just great!"

Matt was so excited, he ran to the kitchen and grabbed a wooden cutting board. And just as he'd seen all the kung fu stars do, Matt attempted to break the thick board in two. With his head. *"Hhhhhiiiyyyyyaaaa!"* he shouted. But the cutting board stayed in one piece. "Ow!" He looked a little dazed and started walking in circles.

"Son, you okay?" Mr. McGuire asked, running over. "Son, listen. I think we're gonna write the best essay this magazine's ever seen."

Matt rubbed his forehead and looked at his father. "Essay?" he said, halfheartedly. "Well, you know, writing isn't my best subject."

Mr. McGuire put his arm around Matt. "Not to worry, son. You're sitting with the guy who won a free trip to Washington, D.C., in 1976 for his brilliant Bicentennial essay,

'America: It's More Than Just Amber Waves of Grain.'"

"Uh, sounds great, Dad," Matt said, totally unconvinced. "Just great."

"I'll get it!" Lizzie shouted at the sound of the doorbell. She ran downstairs to open the front door and was shocked to see . . .

Gordo! "Hey," he said, the same way he did every day he came over.

Lizzie's eyes flew open wide. "You, you, you can't be here!" she said, frantically.

"And yet I *am* here." Gordo brushed by her. "Your mom said we were going to the mall."

"Hi, Mr. McGuire. Hey, Matt," Gordo said as he walked into the kitchen. He sat down at the kitchen table and made himself at home. "Hi, Mrs. McGuire," he said.

"Hey, Gordo," she replied with a smile.

Just then, Miranda walked downstairs and

into the kitchen. "Hey, Mrs. McGuire, I just called my mom. She's cool with the whole mall thing."

Then, out of the corner of her eye, Miranda noticed Gordo. "Uh, why are *you* here?" she asked, placing her hands on her hips.

"I invited him," said Mrs. McGuire. She poured Gordo a glass of juice.

"When?" the girls asked at the same time.

"When I just called," Gordo said.

"I figured if you guys needed school supplies for a project, so does Gordo," Mrs. McGuire said.

Miranda shot Lizzie a look of panic. This was a hitch in the plan they hadn't thought of! Lizzie had to come up with something fast. There was no way in the world that she was buying a bra in front of Gordo!

"Oh, Gordo doesn't need any school supplies," Lizzie said, biting her nails.

"What school project?" Gordo asked.

"You're not in that class," Miranda said quickly.

"But I'm in all of your classes," Gordo answered. "Except gym."

"Well, then, that's it!" Lizzie said, clapping her hands together. "It's a very secret, special gym project that only Miranda and I need to go shopping for."

"Yeah," Miranda agreed. "A secret gym project." She hid her face with her hands and shook her head. This was getting ugly.

Lizzie's back was up against the fridge. All eyes in the room were on her.

Mrs. McGuire took a step forward, folding her arms across her chest. "What's the project, Lizzie?"

Miranda spoke up. "It's a . . ."

Mrs. McGuire held up her hand, traffic-cop style. "I asked Lizzie," she said, taking another step toward her daughter. Matt and Mr. McGuire exchanged glances.

Lizzie tried to back up but there was no room to move. Lizzie looked at Miranda for help, but her friend just shrugged her shoulders.

"What do you need at the mall, Lizzie?" Mrs. McGuire demanded.

i'd like to see a lawyer!

"Lizzie?" Mrs. McGuire asked again.

Lizzie twirled her hair.

"Tell . . . me . . . the . . . truth. . . ." said Mrs. McGuire. Lizzie wondered if everyone in the room heard her mother's voice the same way she did—as if she were in slow motion and underwater. Lizzie looked at Miranda. Then at Gordo. Then at her mother.

Everyone was staring at her. She couldn't think fast enough—so she cracked.

"A BRA, OKAY?" Lizzie practically shouted. "I want a bra! A bra! *We* want a bra!"

The kitchen was quieter than the mall after closing. Lizzie couldn't even look at Miranda. Now she'd done it! Now her mom would go with them to the mall, for sure. She didn't know what to say, so she just repeated, "I want a bra! A bra. A bra. A bra." She said it over and over, like a zombie.

"Ewww!" Matt shouted. "That's disgusting!"

Miranda held her head in her hands. This was totally out of control.

"A bra?" Mr. McGuire said out loud. "Honey, isn't she kind of young for that?"

"Absolutely not!" Mrs. McGuire hurried over and drew her daughter into a hug. Lizzie smiled at her weakly. "And I should have thought of this weeks ago. What was I thinking? I would be delighted to take you girls shopping. Let me get my purse."

Mrs. McGuire was so excited! She had been preparing for this moment since Lizzie was born. As she headed toward the closet, Gordo stopped her.

"Mrs. McGuire?" he said, looking at his sneakers. "Suddenly, I don't want to go to the mall with you guys anymore."

"That's okay," she sang, happily shuffling Lizzie and Miranda out the door. "You're uninvited."

CHAPTER THREE

The front door closed, and the kitchen was silent. Mr. McGuire stared at Matt and Gordo.

"Well . . . how about those Mets? Huh, guys?" asked Mr. McGuire, gently punching each kid in the arm.

"I don't care," Matt said, with his head in his hands. "I'm just glad we don't have to talk about bras anymore."

Gordo jumped out of his chair. "I, uh . . . I have to go home and do something," he said quickly. "Anything. Anything but this."

He started toward the door, but Mr. McGuire stopped him. "Uh, Gordo, maybe you could stick around and help us with Matt's contest entry?"

"Yeah, I'm Jet Li's sidekick in his next movie," Matt explained, pulling the magazine ad out of his back pocket to show Gordo.

Gordo thought for a moment. "I could go home and get my camera," he suggested. After all, he didn't have anything better to do now that his trip to the mall was canceled.

"That's a great idea!" Matt gave the air around him a vicious karate chop.

"All right, I'll be back in ten minutes," Gordo said and he headed out the front door.

Mr. McGuire watched as his son gave the fridge a karate kick. Matt's shoe flew off.

"Buddy, I thought we were gonna write an essay?" Mr. McGuire said.

Matt put his arm around his father. "Dad," he said. "Let's call that Plan B."

Mrs. McGuire was the first one to step into the lingerie department. She was so excited to help the girls choose their first bras, she barely noticed that they were ten feet behind her.

"You cracked like an egg," Miranda whispered to Lizzie.

"I got us here, didn't I?" Lizzie shot back.

"Yeah, with your *mom*," Miranda said. She shook her hair forward in a vain attempt to hide her face. What if someone cool saw her shopping with Lizzie's mother? Total disaster.

The girls were trying so hard not to be noticed that they didn't see the tall saleswoman come up behind them. "Can I help you two with something?" she asked.

Lizzie and Miranda froze, but Mrs. McGuire swooped in. "Yes, hi. We are shopping for their first bras," she said.

Lizzie couldn't tell if it was just her imagination, or if her mom was shouting as though she were at a First Bra Pep Rally.

"This is so cool!" Mrs. McGuire said, hugging the girls. Then she turned to the saleswoman and asked, "Where's the Little Miss section?"

"Over there by the footie pajamas," the saleswoman answered helpfully.

Both Lizzie and Miranda turned purple with humiliation. It was bad enough Lizzie needed her mother to go bra shopping, but now they all had to shop in the footie-pajama area. This wasn't exactly the sophisticated shopping spree they had in mind.

Mrs. McGuire was off like a shot. "Okay, great, thanks. C'mon, girls," she said at the top of her lungs, already halfway to the Little Miss section. Miranda and Lizzie trailed behind, mortified.

"Mom?" Lizzie whispered. "Do you think maybe we could be a little more quiet about this?"

"About what?" he mother demanded at top volume.

Lizzie sighed. She knew her mom was only trying to be helpful . . . it wasn't her fault that she didn't have a clue. "Oh, nothing," Lizzie said, wanting to kick over a nearby mannequin.

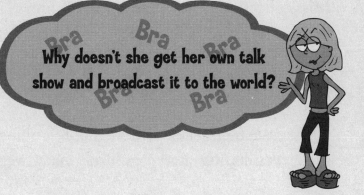

Why doesn't she get her own talk show and broadcast it to the world?

Mrs. McGuire had hit the jackpot. She was very focused as she rummaged through all the bras in the Little Miss underwear collection. She was singing to herself as she picked out as many bras as her hands could hold. Lizzie and Miranda hid behind the pajamas.

"Can we ditch her?" Miranda begged. "Please."

"No," Lizzie said, knowing how much it would hurt her mom's feelings. "But we *can* pretend to get lost. Come on!"

Miranda grinned as Lizzie grabbed her hand and yanked her away from the Little Miss collection. They were going to run as far away as was humanly possible. In their desperate attempt to escape, they smashed into an innocent bystander carrying a flannel nightgown.

"Excuse me," they said without looking, their eyes staring at the ground. They were about to make another break for it, when they heard a familiar voice.

"Lizzie? Miranda?" the voice said. They looked up.

"Mr. Coopersmith?" Lizzie said unbelievingly. Her very cute English teacher was standing right in front of her!

No. Not happening. I am not running into my cute English teacher in the you-know-what department. Shouldn't he be home, handling grammar emergencies?

Mr. Coopersmith flashed his million-dollar smile at the girls. "I'm just buying a birthday present for my wife," he said, showing off the flannel nightie draped over his arm.

Lizzie stood there and stared at her teacher with a nervous smile. Miranda was about to say something when a voice called out from the other side of the store.

"Hey, girls, I found some really cute things for you." Mrs. McGuire caught up with them, her arms overflowing with different-colored bras.

Miranda squeezed Lizzie's arm in panic. Lizzie wanted to disappear.

"Oh, hello, Mr. Coopersmith," said Mrs. McGuire, noticing her daughter's teacher. "How're you doing?"

"I'm good . . . good," he said.

"Well, it's good to see you," she said. Then she piled the girls' arms with the bras she was carrying and instructed them to go to the dressing room to try everything on.

"Let's go," Lizzie said to Miranda. The two girls trudged toward the fitting room as if going off to an execution.

CHAPTER FOUR

Back at the McGuire household, Mr. McGuire was scribbling furiously on a pad of paper. He had a ton of great ideas for Matt's Jet Li essay. Despite his earlier apprehension, he was really starting to get into this! Gordo, meanwhile, was mapping out the living room for good places to shoot in an effort to forget the bra incident.

"Where's Matt?" Gordo asked.

"Upstairs, getting ready," Mr. McGuire said

distractedly. He was concentrating on the finishing touches of his work. When it was perfect, he handed the pad over to Gordo. "Take a look. I've got some interview questions for you."

"What's your name?" Gordo read aloud from the list. "How old are you? Where do you go to school?"

"That is my absolute favorite," said Mr. McGuire, dreamily.

Gordo cocked an eyebrow. "Uh, these are some really great questions, Mr. McGuire," he lied. "But, you know, there . . . there are some other ways we could go."

Just then, Matt jumped down the stairs. *"Hhhhhiiiyyyyyaaaa!"* he shouted.

He was wearing a pair of white pajamas, with one of his father's black ties cinched around his waist.

"Looking good, Matt," Gordo said. "So what I was thinking is, we shoot a couple of cool establishing shots. First, Matt raking in the Zen garden . . ."

"We don't have a Zen garden," Mr. McGuire pointed out. "And what about my questions?"

Gordo didn't know how to tell Mr. McGuire that his questions wouldn't even win a penmanship contest. He wracked his brain to come up with a way to break it to him gently. "Mr. McGuire, these questions are very . . ."

"Boring!" Matt shouted. Gordo gave him a look. So much for letting Mr. McGuire down easy.

"Boring?" Mr. McGuire looked shocked.

Gordo scratched his head. "Mr. McGuire, if Matt's gonna win this thing, we need something big. Something that is gonna set his entry apart from the rest."

"Okay, Gordo," Mr. McGuire said. "What would you suggest?"

Gordo took a deep breath. "I think we need to shoot our own martial arts movie."

"You are way too cool to be Lizzie's friend," Matt said, giving Gordo a high five.

Mr. McGuire just shook his head and sighed.

Back at the mall, Lizzie and Miranda were safely tucked behind the curtains of their dressing rooms. Mrs. McGuire had left them alone so she could continue shopping for the perfect bras. At least, now, they had a little privacy, even though neither one of them could bring herself to try on any of the bras.

"Okay, so getting lost didn't work," Lizzie said. "What'll we do now?"

"Well, we're supposed to be adults, right?" Miranda answered from behind her curtain.

"So?" Lizzie asked.

"So, tell her we want to shop alone," Miranda said.

Lizzie put her hands on her hips and talked to the wall that separated her from Miranda. "If you're so adult, why don't *you* tell her?" she asked.

"Are you insane?" Miranda demanded. "*You* tell her!"

Lizzie shook her head. "*I'm* not telling her!"

"Telling me what?" Mrs. McGuire asked, pulling Lizzie's curtain aside.

"Mom!" Lizzie griped. "I could have been changing!"

Mrs. McGuire laughed. "Oh, honey, it's just us girls here."

"No, it's not!" Lizzie shouted.

Mrs. McGuire didn't get Lizzie's hint. "Well, here, I just brought you some more stuff to try on," she said. Lizzie wondered if there was a bra in the store that her mother *hadn't* picked up.

"We can find things on our own." Lizzie turned her back on her mother.

"Okay, well, I'm just trying to help." Mrs. McGuire hung the bras on the hook inside the dressing room.

Lizzie grabbed all the bras off the hook. Then she took a deep breath and said, "We don't need your help."

"Okay." Mrs. McGuire's voice was patient. "What *do* you need?"

"We need you to leave us alone, okay?" Lizzie snapped, dropping the bras on the chair in the corner of her dressing room.

Mrs. McGuire held her breath for a moment. Lizzie couldn't bear to look at the expression on her mother's face, so she just kept talking. "You're always going on about what little adults we are, and when we try to act like adults, you treat us like we're children! We're not children, okay? We're just not!"

When Lizzie was through, she plopped down on the chair, sitting right on all the bras. Mrs. McGuire just stood there, staring at her daughter. She was very quiet as she fished around in her purse. When she found what she was looking for, Mrs. McGuire gave Lizzie a very forced smile and said, "Okay. Here's forty dollars. I'll be in the food court. You come find me when you're all finished."

By the time Lizzie looked up, her mother had already gone.

Miranda popped her head out of her dressing room. Lizzie stared at one of the bras that had fallen to the floor. She felt like kicking it straight to the footie-pajama section.

"That wasn't exactly the way I pictured the adult conversation between you and your mom," Miranda said.

"Well, me neither," Lizzie said sadly. Then she added in a firmer voice, "But a girl's gotta do what a girl's gotta do."

Miranda eyed the money in Lizzie's hand. Then she smiled and said, "On the plus side, we're alone in the mall with your mother's cash."

Who says money can't buy happiness?

Lizzie leaned against the mirror in the dressing room. "I know I got exactly what I wanted," she said with a sigh. "So, why don't I feel better?"

Miranda rolled her eyes and dragged Lizzie out of the dressing room. Now they were free to shop to their hearts' content.

"This is so much easier without my mother hanging around," Lizzie said.

"Exactly," Miranda agreed.

The girls stared at the rack blankly. There must have been a million things to choose from.

"So, what are we looking for?" Miranda asked.

Lizzie shrugged. "I dunno," she admitted. "I thought *you* knew."

"I thought I did, too." Miranda's voice sounded slightly panicked. "But there are all these numbers and letters. 32's, 34's, 36's, A's, B's, C's!"

Lizzie decided to approach this logically. "Well, I mean, Kate owns one, right? How hard can it be?" she asked.

"You're right." Miranda's voice was dubious, but she added, "If Kate and her friends can do it, *we* can do it."

CHAPTER FIVE

Back in the imaginary Zen garden, the camera was focused on Matt and Gordo. The two actors assumed their very best kung fu stance.

"You should never have come back here, Matthew-san. Now I will be forced to destroy you," Gordo said.

The boys had the moves down perfectly. Gordo had even worked it out so their mouths moved before any sound came out— just like in dubbed kung fu movies.

"You cannot destroy what you cannot catch!" Matt said. He bent his knees and crossed his arms, showing he was ready to strike. Matt looked at Gordo. Gordo looked at Matt. And then . . .

"AAAAAAAAAAAAHHHHHHHH!" Gordo shouted as the two began their staged battle.

Matt revved up his arms and made high-pitched noises. Gordo tried to block Matt's chops with his legs. But it was no use. Matt was the master. He quickly won the battle and brought Gordo to his knees. As Gordo keeled over, Matt placed his foot upon his opponent in victory. It was beautiful.

Matt turned sharply to the camera and said, "That's what Jet Li's sidekick does!"

"AND CUT!" Gordo shouted from under Matt's foot.

* * *

Swimming in an unknown sea of bras, the girls were clearly drowning.

Suddenly, Lizzie saw something terrible out of the corner of her eye. "Oh, no!" she whispered in horror. Standing on the other side of the bra rack were Kate and Claire. And they were staring right at Lizzie and Miranda.

"What are you guys doing here?" Kate sneered.

"You must be lost," Claire added. "The dork section is on the *first* floor."

is there some kind of rule that Kate and her posse have to witness every moment of misery in my life?

Stay cool, Lizzie told herself. "We're shopping," she said.

"Yeah, shopping," Miranda added, pretending to pick out some bras.

Kate and Claire smirked at each other. "For what?" Kate asked.

"They don't carry Underoos here." Claire burst out laughing at her own joke.

Before either Lizzie or Miranda had a chance to reply, Claire's mother strode into the lingerie department. "Claire!" she called. "Kate!"

Miranda laughed. "I can't believe you're shopping with Claire's mom."

"Yeah," Lizzie added quickly. "We don't have to shop with *our* moms."

"Claire, there you are," said Mrs. Miller. "Oh, hello, Lizzie. Hi, Miranda. I haven't seen you guys around for a while. Where are your moms?"

This was Lizzie's moment to embarrass Kate and Claire. She had been waiting for this for what seemed like forever. "Oh, we get to shop by ourselves," Lizzie said proudly. She glared at Kate and Claire.

"By yourselves?" asked Mrs. Miller. "So, do you need any help?"

"N-n-n-no," Lizzie answered. "Nope, no help needed here!"

"We're fine," Miranda agreed.

"Okay, then. Tell your moms I said hi." Mrs. Miller gave a little wave as she headed out of the store.

Claire and Kate followed behind Mrs. Miller. But right before they left, Claire turned around to make one last obnoxious comment. "Oh, the footie pajamas are over there in the toddler section."

"Good one!" Kate said. She and Claire laughed all the way out of the store.

Lizzie heaved a sigh of relief. At least Kate and Claire were gone. Now more than ever, the girls were psyched to be alone again. But as Lizzie and Miranda turned toward the rack of bras, they realized it was time to face the facts.

"We are so lost," Miranda said.

"I have no clue what I'm doing," Lizzie admitted.

i need Mr. Snuggles.

"This was a total mistake." Miranda bit her lip. "Maybe we're not ready."

Lizzie stopped pretending to choose a bra. She took a deep breath and ran her hand through her blond hair. "You know, I don't need a salesperson, and I don't need Mrs.

Miller," Lizzie said. And then it dawned on her. "Miranda, I think I need my mom."

"That's the best idea you've had all day," Miranda agreed.

For the first time that day, the girls felt sure of something. They made their way to the food court faster than Lizzie could say "bra."

Meanwhile, back in show business, Gordo angled the lens close-up on Mr. McGuire.

"Only when the student can take the pebble from the master," Mr. McGuire said awkwardly, reading from the script Gordo had given him, "does the student become . . . Jet Li's sidekick."

Mr. McGuire extended his arm. He slowly opened the palm of his hand to reveal a small pebble. Matt grabbed it from the master's hand.

"Yes!" Matt shouted as he did a victory dance around the backyard.

"Okay. Cut, cut!" Gordo yelled, frustrated. "Um, sir," he said, walking up to Mr. McGuire, "this is the climax of the movie. So it's kinda important that you stick to the script."

Mr. McGuire gave Gordo a strange look. "I did."

"No, you have to close your hand when Matt tries to take the stone. You gotta make it a little hard."

Mr. McGuire adjusted his glasses and sighed. "You know, I'm sorry, Gordo, but I don't think a kung fu rip-off is as effective as a well-written and grammatically perfect essay."

"What are you talking about, Dad?" Matt asked, still victory-dancing all around the backyard. "It's totally better."

Mr. McGuire put his hands in his pockets and kicked at the dirt with his foot. "Well, you know, you two seem to have a better feel for this stuff than I do, so I'll just leave it to you," he said, bowing his head, and skulking into the house. Once inside, he watched the boys through the French doors. As he stared, the two tried hard to figure out how to make the scene work best. The more Mr. McGuire watched the boys, the more he realized how serious they were about this movie. He paced around the living room a few times. Then, he picked up the telephone and began to dial.

"Hey, David? It's Sam. I need a favor," Mr. McGuire said, looking outside again. He spoke quietly into the receiver. "Are you still teaching kung fu?"

Outside, Gordo was having a hard time. He had way too many roles to play, and it was getting the best of him. First, he had to be an actor and do kung fu moves with Matt. But he also had to film the video! It was exhausting. The boys attempted to get it right several times. But something always went wrong. Either the pebble went flying out of Gordo's hands when Matt tried to snatch it, or they were doing the scene, completely unaware that they were out of the frame of the camera lens. The last straw came when the tripod fell over, sending the camera flying.

"Aargh!" Gordo ran over to pick up the fallen camera.

"Gordo, we've done this scene seven times already," Matt complained. "Aren't we done yet?"

"I'm sorry, Matt," Gordo said. "But it was a lot easier with your father helping."

Matt tightened his black belt and hiked up his pajama bottoms. Enough was enough! "Then let's go get him," he said.

But they didn't have to. Because Mr. McGuire had just walked up behind them.

"Mr. McGuire, we really need your help here," Gordo pleaded.

"Guys, I told you, I really don't know much about this kung fu stuff," Mr. McGuire said. "But I know someone who does."

With that, a strange man entered the backyard. He was in full kung fu regalia and wasn't even wearing shoes. The boys stared at him in awe. Gordo thought he looked familiar, but just couldn't place where he'd seen him before. Was it on television? He couldn't put his finger on it.

"Hello, young grasshopper," the man said calmly.

Matt looked around to find the grasshopper the man was talking about. Then he looked at his dad quizzically. "Dad, why is he calling me grasshopper?"

Mr. McGuire chuckled. "Just go with it, son."

The man stared hard into Matt's eyes.

"Your father tells me you wish to be a martial artist," he said.

"Yeah, Jet Li's sidekick," Matt answered, hopefully.

"I have much to teach you," the man said seriously. "But you must be willing to learn."

Matt shrugged his shoulders. "Uh, okay," he answered.

CHAPTER SIX

Mrs. McGuire sat alone in the food court. She sipped her soda, and stared blankly down at her nails. Then she looked up and was surprised to see Lizzie and Miranda coming up to her table. "Hi, girls," she said, smiling weakly. "Did you finish your shopping?"

The girls exchanged looks.

"Not exactly." Miranda put her hands in the back pockets of her jeans.

"It didn't really go the way we planned," Lizzie added quietly.

Mrs. McGuire motioned for the girls to sit down. "Listen, I'm really sorry—" she started to say.

"You know what, Mom?" Lizzie interrupted.

"No, let me finish," Mrs. McGuire said, putting down her soda. "I remember when I was thirteen and my mom took me shopping. She would do everything possible to embarrass me. And I promised myself I would never act like that with my own daughter."

Lizzie put her hand on her mom's shoulder and said, "Mom, you didn't act that way."

"You're right," said Mrs. McGuire. "I was *worse*. You *are* becoming adults, and I should've let you just do it on your own. And I'm sorry."

"No, you *really* shouldn't have," Miranda said, remembering the enormous and intimidating rack of bras she had faced.

"And we're not adults," Lizzie added.

Miranda rolled her eyes. "Not even close."

Mrs. McGuire laughed and slid out of her chair to give the girls a hug.

Lizzie looked at her mother seriously. "And you know that temper tantrum I just threw in the dressing room? Not exactly adult material. So I'm really sorry."

"Me, too," said Miranda.

Lizzie smiled at her mom. "I guess the adult thing to do sometimes is ask for help."

"You didn't buy anything, did you?" Mrs. McGuire asked happily.

Lizzie shook her head. "Nope," she said.

"Nada," Miranda agreed.

"Well, then let's go shopping!" Mrs. McGuire hooked her elbows, and the three walked off arm in arm. Lizzie knew she had done the right thing. She also knew she had an extra forty bucks to spend at the mall.

"Oh, Give me my forty dollars," Mrs. McGuire said quickly.

They forget to sign field trip forms, forget you don't like liverwurst, but they never forget when they give you cash.

At long last, the McGuire backyard was beginning to look like the set of a real kung fu movie. The mystery man had taught everyone some official moves—even Mr. McGuire practiced a few.

Matt squared off against the mystery man. His opponent tried to block his move, but Matt chopped and kicked with such power and force, that he eventually chased his master all around the lawn. It took some work, but eventually the man was defeated. He bowed his head and said, "Class dismissed."

Gordo stood behind the camera, getting each of these expert moves on film while Mr. McGuire watched the final scene unfold. The mystery master stared at Matt and quietly said, "When you can snatch the pebble from my hand, it will be time for you to be Jet Li's sidekick."

Gordo tightened the shot on the master's hand. Matt tried to swipe the pebble, but the master closed his fist. "Master?" Matt asked. "Why do you close your hand?"

"You have many questions, grasshopper," the master said slowly. "But I have a question for you, Matt."

Mr. McGuire, armed with his pad of paper, flashed the master the list of questions he had worked on earlier.

The master read from the notes as he faced the camera. "What is it that qualifies you to be the best choice to become Jet Li's side-kick?"

Matt thought for a moment. "Well, because I'm smart and funny and I do my own stunts!" And with that, he whipped his hand from behind his back and snatched the pebble out of the master's hand. He was so quick, the master never saw a thing.

"How did you do that?" the man asked, amazed.

Matt held the pebble high above his head. "Whoo-hoo!" he shouted. "Who's the grasshopper now?"

"And cut!" Gordo shouted. "That's a wrap!"

The defeated opponent bowed to Mr. McGuire and quietly said that his work there was done.

"High five, Dad!" Matt shouted. "You're the coolest!"

The master walked into the house. Gordo wasn't sure if he was tired, or he actually saw the mystery man fade away and disappear in the middle of the living room!

"Mr. McGuire, who was that man?" Gordo asked in a daze.

"Gordo," Mr. McGuire said. "I've known him all my life. He's like a brother to me."

The guys all went inside to relax. Show business was exhausting!

Later that night, Lizzie was curled up on her bed, twirling the phone cord as she recapped the day's events with Gordo and Miranda. "I can't believe you spent all afternoon with Matt and my dad!" she said to Gordo, rolling her eyes. Her day might have been humiliating, but it wasn't nearly as horrible as hanging out with her little brother.

"Hey, Matt and your dad are pretty cool. We made a kung fu movie," Gordo said. "And considering the alternative, I'd say it was a good choice."

Lizzie thought about her day. She replayed everything in her mind, from running into her English teacher in the bra department, to being harassed by the ever-nauseating Kate and Claire. She recalled how she had been totally clueless about how to pick a bra and how she had hurt her mom's feelings. It was pretty disastrous, but she had survived! She cradled the phone to her ear and hugged Mr. Snuggles. "Well, I don't think we'll be having any more girl-only shopping trips for quite a while," she said.

"Yeah, Gordo," Miranda interjected with a laugh. "It's safe to go to the mall with us again."

"Cool," he said. "But when you start talking about shopping for school supplies, let me know when you mean school supplies, or *'school supplies.'*"

"Deal!" Lizzie and Miranda giggled.

My work here is done.

The next morning, Mr. McGuire was going about his regular business. He sipped his coffee as he flipped through the newspaper. He was in the middle of the sports section when the phone rang. He waited a couple of rings, since Lizzie usually ran to answer the phone first, but it just kept on ringing. "Hello?" he said into the receiver, putting down the newspaper. "Yes, this is Matt McGuire's father . . . you're calling from the Jet Li Sidekick contest?"

Mr. McGuire listened to the man on the other end of the line. He could barely believe what he was hearing, so he repeated it to make sure. "He won? Matt's gonna be Jet Li's sidekick?"

The man on the other end of the line confirmed the fact that Matt's video was by far the best entry they had received. Mr. McGuire politely and quietly thanked the caller. Then he calmly returned the phone back to its cradle.

"Ahhhhh!" Mr. McGuire screamed. Then he did a victory dance around the living room! After all, his son was about to star in a movie. Plus, Mr. McGuire knew it was his excellent question-writing skills that *really* won Matt the job!

GET INSIDE HER HEAD

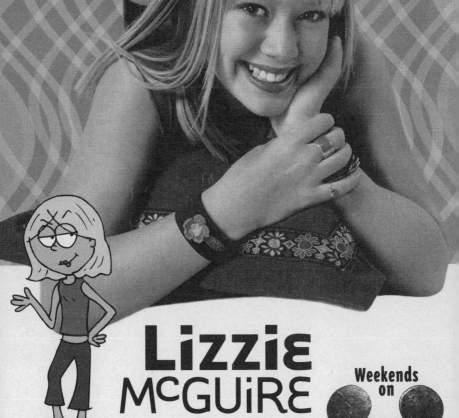

Lizzie McGUiRE

Weekends on Disney CHANNEL℠

A Disney Channel Original Series

©Disney

Visit Lizzie @ ZoogDisney.com

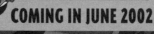